For Kelli Huffman, a true friend; and in memory of her Nana,
Libbye G. Prawde

First edition 2008

Library of Congress Cataloging-in-Publication Data is available.

Library of Congress Catalog Card Number 2007940978

ISBN 978-0-7636-3614-2

2 4 6 8 10 9 7 5 3 1

Printed in China

This book was typeset in Triplex Serif Light.
The illustrations were done in ink and acrylic, combined digitally.

Candlewick Press
2067 Massachusetts Avenue
Cambridge, Massachusetts 02140

visit us at www.candlewick.com

CECE BELL

BEE-WIGGED

CANDLEWICK PRESS
CAMBRIDGE, MASSACHUSETTS

Jerry Bee loved people.

But people did not love Jerry Bee.

For one thing, he was a bee.

For another, he was the most enormous bee anyone had ever seen.

A sting from a bee Jerry's size would really hurt.

So people stayed away.

It's true that Jerry was quite large. But he had never stung anyone in his entire life.

In fact, he had tried hard to make friends.

But nothing worked.

One morning, Jerry saw an old wig lying on the sidewalk. *Why not?* thought Jerry. And he put the wig on his head.

Just then, he heard a bus driver shout, "Young man, you're late for school!" The bus driver stopped her bus, opened the door, and hollered, "Get in!"

Jerry got on the bus.

As Jerry looked at himself in the mirror, he had a wonderful thought: If he looked like a boy instead of a bee, maybe people would finally like him!

When the bus stopped, Jerry made a beeline for the school. He couldn't wait to make friends with all the people inside!

Jerry entered the first classroom he could find.

"Excuse me, ma'am," he said. "My name is Jerry, and
I would love to join your wonderful class. And might
I add that you are looking quite lovely today?"

Miss Swann was the first friend Jerry made that day.

The students really liked
Jerry, too.

He was helpful,

funny,

artistic,

and generous.

He was even a terrific speller.

By the end of the day, Jerry Bee had more friends
than he had ever had in his life.

So Jerry decided to come to school every day.
And every day, he made more friends.

One day, he helped the janitor mop.

The next day, he complimented the lunch ladies on their food.

Jerry inspired the cheerleaders with his remarkable team spirit.

He even won over the bus driver.

By the end of the week, everyone loved Jerry so much . . .

that they made him the grand marshal of the annual school parade!

Jerry Bee was ecstatic. He couldn't believe how much the wig had changed his life.

Then the wind started blowing. Hard.

The wind blew Jerry's wig right off his head!

He tried to catch it, but . . .

he was too late.

Everyone saw Jerry without the wig, and everyone saw that he was the most enormous bee they had ever seen.

It was the wig!

Everyone was quiet. And then . . .

"HOORAY for Jerry Bee! HOORAY

for Wiglet! HIP, HIP, HOORAY!"

everyone shouted.

It was the best day of Jerry Bee's life.
At last he could be himself *and* have friends.

And Wiglet would be his best friend forever.

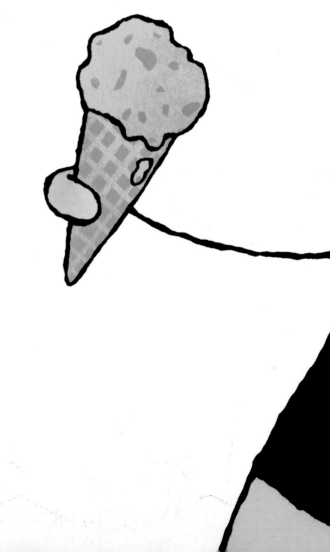